ᴅᴋ READERS

Level 4

Days of the Knights
Volcanoes and Other Natural Disasters
Secrets of the Mummies
Pirates! Raiders of the High Seas
Horse Heroes
Trojan Horse
Micro Monsters
Going for Gold!
Extreme Machines
Flying Ace: The Story of Amelia
　Earhart
Robin Hood
Black Beauty
Free at Last! The Story of
　Martin Luther King, Jr.
Joan of Arc
Spooky Spinechillers
Welcome to The Globe! The
　Story of Shakespeare's Theater
Antarctic Adventure
Space Station: Accident on Mir
Atlantis: The Lost City?
Dinosaur Detectives
Danger on the Mountain: Scaling
　the World's Highest Peaks
Crime Busters
The Story of Muhammad Ali
First Flight: The Story of the
　Wright Brothers
D-Day Landings: The Story of
　the Allied Invasion
Solo Sailing
Thomas Edison: The Great Inventor
Dinosaurs! Battle of the Bones
LEGO: Race for Survival
NFL: NFL's Greatest Upsets
NFL: Rumbling Running Backs
NFL: Super Bowl!
MLB: Strikeout Kings
MLB: Super Shortstops: Jeter,
　Nomar, and A-Rod
MLB: The Story of the New York
　Yankees
MLB: The World of Baseball

MLB: October Magic: All the Best
　World Series!
WCW: Feel the Sting
WCW: Going for Goldberg
JLA: Batman's Guide to Crime
　and Detection
JLA: Superman's Guide to the
　Universe
JLA: Aquaman's Guide to the
　Oceans
JLA: Wonder Woman's Book of
　Myths
JLA: Flash's Guide to Speed
JLA: Green Lantern's Guide to
　Great Inventions
The Story of the X-Men: How it all
　Began
Creating the X-Men: How Comic
　Books Come to Life
Spider-Man's Amazing Powers
The Story of Spider-Man
The Incredible Hulk's Book of
　Strength
The Story of the Incredible Hulk
Fantastic Four: Evil Adversaries
Marvel Heroes: Greatest Battles
Transformers: The Awakening
Transformers: The Quest
Transformers: The Unicron Battles
Transformers: The Uprising
Transformers: Megatron Returns
Transformers: Terracon Attack
Star Wars: Galactic Crisis!
Star Wars: Beware the Dark Side
Star Wars: Epic Battles
Graphic Readers: The Terror Trail
Graphic Readers: The Price of
　Victory
Graphic Readers: Curse of the
　Crocodile God
Graphic Readers: Instruments of
　Death
Graphic Readers: Wagon Train
　Adventure

A Note to Parents and Teachers

DK READERS is a compelling program for beginning readers, designed in conjunction with leading literacy experts, including Dr. Linda Gambrell, Professor of Education at Clemson University. Dr. Gambrell has served as president of the National Reading Conference and the College Reading Association, and has recently been elected to serve as president of the International Reading Association.

Beautiful illustrations and superb full-color photographs combine with engaging, easy-to-read stories to offer a fresh approach to each subject in the series.

Each DK READER is guaranteed to capture a child's interest while developing his or her reading skills, general knowledge, and love of reading.

The five levels of DK READERS are aimed at different reading abilities, enabling you to choose the books that are exactly right for your child:

Pre-level 1: Learning to read
Level 1: Beginning to read
Level 2: Beginning to read alone
Level 3: Reading alone
Level 4: Proficient readers

The "normal" age at which a child begins to read can be anywhere from three to eight years old. Adult participation through the lower levels is very helpful in providing encouragement, discussing storylines, and sounding out unfamiliar words.

No matter which level you select, you can be sure that you are helping your child learn to read, then read to learn!

LONDON, NEW YORK, MUNICH,
MELBOURNE, AND DELHI

Editor Kate Simkins
Designers Cathy Tincknell
and John Kelly
Senior Editor Catherine Saunders
Brand Manager Lisa Lanzarini
Publishing Manager Simon Beecroft
Category Publisher Alex Allan
Production Editor Siu Chan
Production Controller Amy Bennett

Reading Consultant
Linda Gambrell

First American Edition, 2008
Published in the United States by
DK Publishing
375 Hudson Street
New York, New York 10014

08 09 10 11 12 10 9 8 7 6 5 4 3 2 1

Copyright © 2008 Dorling Kindersley Limited

Published in Great Britain by Dorling Kindersley Limited.

DK books are available at special discounts for bulk purchases for
sales promotion, premiums, fund-raising, or educational use.
For details contact: DK Publishing Special Markets,
375 Hudson Street, New York, NY 10014

A Cataloging-in-Publication record for this book is available from
the Library of Congress.

ISBN 978-0-75663-851-1 (paperback)
ISBN 978-0-75663-852-8 (hardcover)

Hi-res workflow proofed by Media Development and Printing Ltd., UK.
Printed and bound in China by L-Rex Printing Co. Ltd.

Discover more at
www.dk.com

Contents

WAGON TRAIN
ADVENTURE

Written by John Kelly
Illustrated by Inklink

Wagon Train Adventure

Sarah's story takes place on the California Trail in 1849. During the 1800s, thousands of people from the eastern United States of America traveled west to California and Oregon, where land was cheap and the climate healthy. Many families sold everything they owned to pay for the trip west because they believed life would be better there. The journey took up to six months and was so hard that some people did not survive it. Turn to page 44 to see a map and a timeline, then let the story begin....

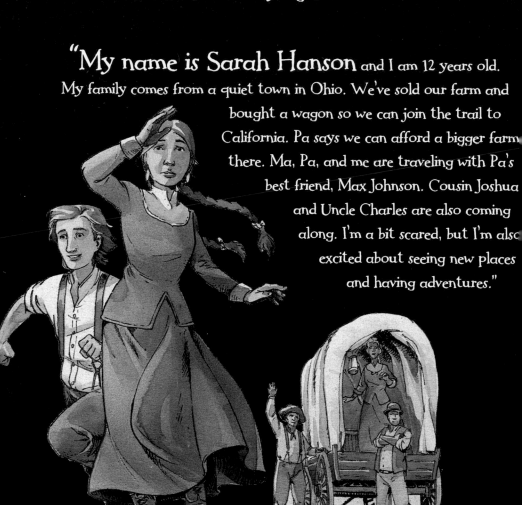

"My name is Sarah Hanson and I am 12 years old. My family comes from a quiet town in Ohio. We've sold our farm and bought a wagon so we can join the trail to California. Pa says we can afford a bigger farm there. Ma, Pa, and me are traveling with Pa's best friend, Max Johnson. Cousin Joshua and Uncle Charles are also coming along. I'm a bit scared, but I'm also excited about seeing new places and having adventures."

Look out for the DID YOU KNOW? facts on every page.

MAY 1849, **INDEPENDENCE, MISSOURI.**

THE TOWN WAS FULL OF PEOPLE. MOST OF US WERE HEADING WEST WITH THE **WAGON TRAINS.**

I COULDN'T BELIEVE MY EYES WHEN I SAW...

...A HUGE **INDIAN** STANDING OUTSIDE A STORE.

*Words in **bold** appear in the glossary on page 45.*

DID YOU KNOW? Wooden statues were often placed outside stores.

DID YOU KNOW? *The people on the wagon trains were called* **emigrants**.

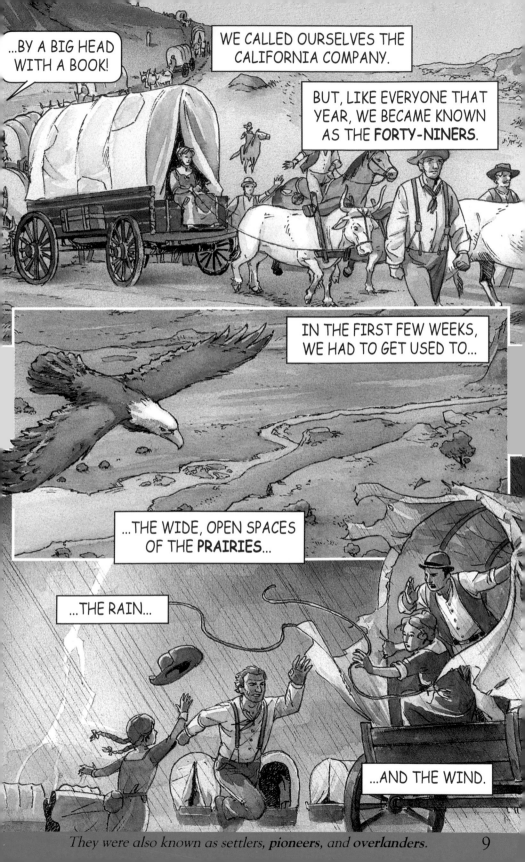

WE WERE OFTEN SOAKED TO THE SKIN...

...EXHAUSTED BY THE LACK OF REST...

...SORE FROM THE ROUGH GOING...

...AND UPSET WHEN OU ANIMALS DIED.

BUT AT THE END OF THE DAY, AFTER WE'D SET UP CAMP FOR THE NIGHT...

...I'D JUST SIT AND STARE UP AT THE STARS.

DID YOU KNOW? When they camped at night, the wagons formed a circle.

DID YOU KNOW? Buffalo, or bison, lived on the prairies of North America.

I RAN...

...AND RAN...

...AS FAST AS I COULD GO.

BUT IT WASN'T FAST ENOUGH...

...EVERYTHING WENT BLACK.

By the 1870s, these large cattle had been almost wiped out by hunting. 13

DID YOU KNOW? Some Indians of the prairies lived in tepees.

These tall, cone-shaped tents were made of animal skins.

DID YOU KNOW? California was part of Mexico until 1848.

WE HAD TO LEAVE ANYTHING THAT WASN'T **ESSENTIAL**.

LUXURIES WERE NOW USELESS TO US...

... AND HAD TO BE THROWN AWAY.

A FEW DAYS OUT OF LARAMIE, THE TRAIN CAME TO HALT.

IS THERE A PROBLEM?

SORT OF!

CHARLES HEARD ABOUT A SHORTCUT BACK AT LARAMIE.

HE THINKS IT'LL KNOCK MILES OFF THE NEXT STAGE.

PA AND MAX THOUGHT IT WAS A MISTAKE.

BUT THEY WERE OUTVOTED.

DID YOU KNOW? Accidents happened often on the trails.

DID YOU KNOW? The emigrants brought foods that would not spoil.

A WEEK LATER, NEAR **INDEPENDENCE ROCK**...

...MAX SENT HIS FIRST MESSAGE BY THE **BONE EXPRESS**.

"I'VE **SCOUTED** OUT THE TRAIL AHEAD."

"IT'S SAFE AS FAR AS **FORT HALL**."

"TRY TO ENJOY THE **FOURTH OF JULY** CELEBRATIONS ON INDEPENDENCE ROCK."

BUT IT WASN'T THE SAME WITHOUT PA AND MAX...

...AND THE JOURNEY SEEMED TO GO ON FOREVER.

These included flour, beans, bacon, and dried fruits and vegetables. 23

DID YOU KNOW? Some people on the trails also got a disease called scurvy.

DID YOU KNOW? Most of the people on the trails were families.

Children often outnumbered the adults on a wagon train.

DID YOU KNOW? Clashes between Indians and settlers were rare.

DID YOU KNOW? *The Indians hunted with bows and arrows.*

MAX WASN'T TOO BADLY WOUNDED.

MR. HENDRIX PATCHED HIM UP...

...AND SAID HE'D BE FINE IN A WEEK OR TWO.

THE WAGON TRAIN VOTED...

...AND WELCOMED MAX BACK AS A HERO!

UNCLE CHARLES WASN'T HAPPY.

The arrows had feathers on one end to help them fly straighter.

DID YOU KNOW? The California Trail crossed the Rocky Mountains.

DID YOU KNOW? The wagon trains traveled about 12–18 miles (20–30 km) a day

WITHOUT THE OTHER WAGONS, THE HILLS SEEMEED STRANGE AND FRIGHTENING.

I GOT A MESSAGE FROM JOSHUA ON THE BONE EXPRESS.

READ IT TO ME, DEAR!

IT WASN'T GOOD NEWS.

EVERY NIGHT, INDIANS WERE SNEAKING INTO CAMP AND SHOOTING OXEN.

UNCLE CHARLES WAS DETERMINED TO STOP THEM...

The wagons were usually pulled by oxen, which are a type of cattle.

DID YOU KNOW? *The oxen pulled the wagons for about 10 hours a day.*

DID YOU KNOW? Indians usually rode on horseback.

Herds of wild horses lived on the prairies.

DID YOU KNOW? By the 1860s, railroads began to replace the wagon trains.

In 1869, the East and West coasts of the US were linked by rail.

THE JOURNEY WEST

Native American tribes (also known as Indians) have lived in what is now the United States for thousands of years, but the first European settlers didn't arrive until the early 1600s. The people in the British colonies (lands owned by Britain) eventually decided they wanted to rule themselves. They declared themselves independent of Britain in 1776 and founded the United States of America.

By the 1800s, the area from the east coast to the Missouri River was settled by Europeans and Americans, but most of the region west of that was uninhabited except by Native American tribes. Only a few maps made by explorers and fur traders existed. With the help of these maps, families started moving west, setting up homes and farms.

As more pioneer families decided to go west, they started traveling in wagon trains because it was safer to go in large groups. They left in the spring and hoped to arrive by the fall, before the snow arrived. The trails took them across rivers, prairies, deserts, and high mountains.

At first, just a few thousand people made the trip west, but after gold was discovered in California in 1848, tens of thousands of settlers traveled a year in the hope of getting rich. This led to clashes with Native Americans, who saw their land and way of life being destroyed.

By 1869, a railroad had been built to link the East and West coasts and the days of the wagon trains came to an end.

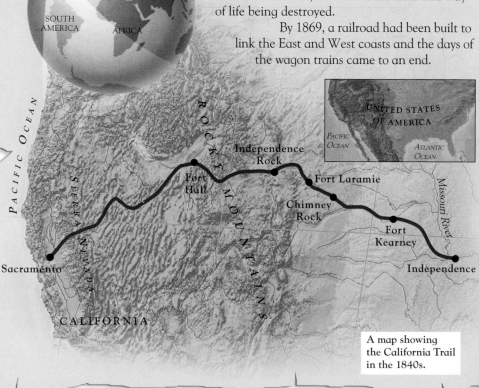

A map showing the California Trail in the 1840s.

GLOSSARY

INDEPENDENCE   PAGE 5
The town of Independence is in the state of Missouri in the American Midwest. It was a "jumping-off" point—a place where emigrants met, organized their wagon trains and set off on the trails. People met at Independence because it was one of the farthest places west people could get to by river boat.

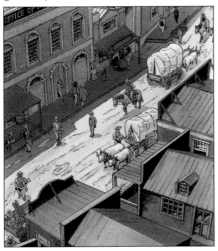

WAGON TRAINS   PAGE 5
Groups of covered wagons traveled in long lines called wagon trains. The number of wagons in a train varied from about six to up to 100.

INDIAN   PAGE 5
American Indians, also called Native Americans, are the people who have lived in North and South America for thousands of years. There were many different Native American tribes living in the United States at the time that Europeans arrived.

MOUNTAIN MAN   PAGE 6
Most mountain men were Europeans who made a living as fur trappers. They hunted wild animals such as bears for their skins and often dressed in the hides of the animals they killed. Mountain men knew the Rocky Mountains and America's western lands well and often worked as guides on the wagon trains.

GRIZZLY BEARS   PAGE 7
These large bears live in the Rocky Mountains. Their brown fur is tipped with gray—"grizzly" means "partly gray."

CAPTAIN   PAGE 7
The wagon trains needed to be highly organized to survive the long journey. The settlers usually elected one of the men as leader, or captain, of the train.

ELECTED   PAGE 8
When people vote to choose a leader, the person who gets the most votes is elected the leader.

GUIDE BOOK PAGE 8

In the 1840s, many emigrants used guidebooks written by settlers who had already traveled the routes to California or Oregon. Most wagon trains, however, also employed a mountain man to guide them on their journey.

EMIGRANTS PAGE 8

Emigrants are people who leave their homes to settle in another country or place.

FORTY-NINERS PAGE 9

The emigrants who traveled to California in 1849 became known as the forty-niners. Gold was discovered in California in 1848, and the following year the number of people on the California Trail greatly increased as people rushed to the gold mines in the hope of getting rich. In 1848, there were only about 400 emigrants, but in 1849, there were about 25,000.

PRAIRIES PAGE 9

The prairies are the grasslands of central North America, east of the Rocky Mountains. The area is also called the Great Plains.

PIONEERS PAGE 9

Pioneers are people who are the first to do something or go somewhere.

OVERLANDERS PAGE 9

California could be reached by sea from the East Coast of America but the trip was long and expensive. Those who went overland by wagon train were often called overlanders.

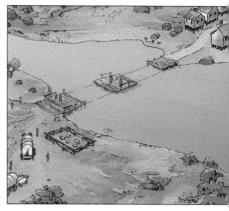

ROPE FERRY PAGE 11

The California Trail took the emigrants across several big rivers. In some places, the water was too deep to drive across and there were no bridges. The only way to cross was on rope ferries—floating wooden platforms pulled by men with ropes. The settlers usually had to pay the men who owned the ferries to use them, although some pioneers built their own ferries.

Buffalo chips   Page 12

There was no wood on the prairies to use as fuel for cooking, so the settlers had to use buffalo dung instead. The dried dung heaps were known as buffalo chips. The chore of collecting buffalo chips was often given to the settler children.

Fort Laramie   Page 17

Fort Laramie was one of several places on the trail where settlers could rest, stock up on fresh food and supplies, and repair their wagons. It was originally built by fur traders as a place to do business with local Native American tribes.

Essential   Page 18

If you can't do without something, it is essential. Essential items for the pioneers would have included food, clothes, and tools for cooking and repairing the wagons.

Luxuries   Page 18

Luxuries are things that are not really necessary. Many settlers dumped pieces of furniture and other items that they didn't really need and were too heavy to carry without slowing down the wagon train.

Independence Rock   Page 23

One of the sights on the trail was Independence Rock, a huge granite rock about 130 feet (40 meters) tall. It got its name because the emigrants attempted to reach the rock by July 4th (Independence Day), having set out in the spring. Many settlers carved their names on the summit of the huge rock.

Bone express   Page 23

The settlers used the bone express to send messages to people on wagon trains behind them on the route. Someone traveling west would write a note and then leave it by the side of the trail in a buffalo skull or a piece of material where it could be easily seen.

Scouted   Page 23

"Scouted" means someone has gone on ahead on a journey and gathered information about the route.

FORT HALL　　　PAGE 23

This trading post was another place where emigrants could stop and get fresh supplies. It was also the place where the California and Oregon trails split. Those going to Oregon went northwest, while those going to California traveled southwest.

FOURTH OF JULY　　　PAGE 23

On the Fourth of July (Independence Day), Americans celebrate the anniversary of the day in 1776 when the United States declared that it would no longer be ruled by Britain.

MOUNTAIN FEVER　　　PAGE 24

The symptoms of mountain fever included a headache, fever, and muscle pains. The illness may have been caused by a bite from an insect  called a tick. It was a deadly disease, but cholera was the most deadly disease on the trail, and few people survived it.

AXLES　　　PAGE 32

Axles are long bars that connect the wheels on a vehicle. A pioneer wagon's axles were made of wood, and sometimes they broke going over bumpy ground.

PASS　　　PAGE 39

A pass is a way through a mountain.

LANDSLIDE　　　PAGE 40

A landslide happens when rocks and dirt fall down the side of a hill or mountain.

FUSE　　　PAGE 41

A fuse is a piece of flammable cord. One end of the cord is lit and the flame travels along its length until it reaches gunpowder at the other end. This sets off an explosion.

Don't miss...

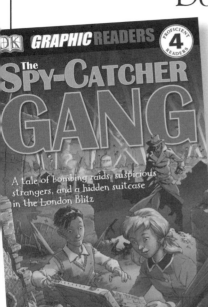

THE SPY-CATCHER GANG
A mysterious tale of bombs, spies, and a hidden suitcase in the London Blitz.

INSTRUMENTS OF DEATH
A gripping story of intrigue and death at the court of the first emperor of China.

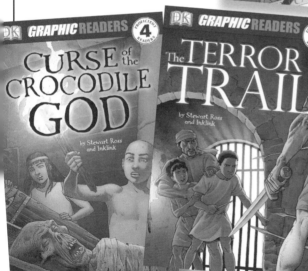

CURSE OF THE CROCODILE GOD
A terrifying tale of tomb robbers in Ancient Egypt.

THE TERROR TRAIL
A breathless tale of faith and justice in Rome's arena of death, the Colosseum.

THE PRICE OF VICTORY
An exciting story of rivalry and sabotage at the Olympic Games in Ancient Greece.

i/09